SOFA STORIES

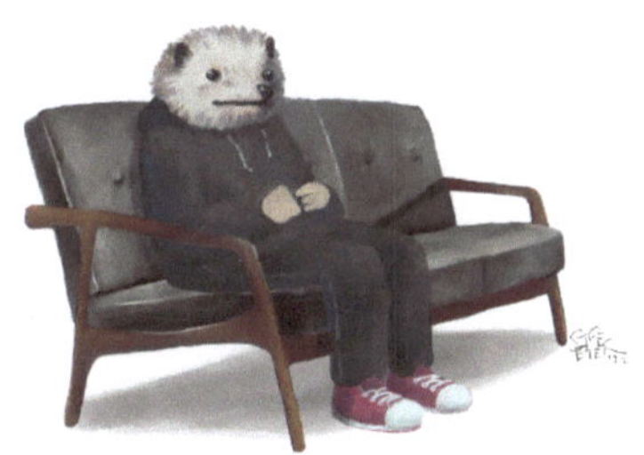

IT FEELS LIKE A CHILDREN'S BOOK, RIGHT?

Published by Studio Yes Yes

Proofread by Christie Baugher and Kio Stark

ISBN: 978-0-9777264-2-4

First printed: December 2022

Hello.

Sofa Stories is a children's book for grownups and grownup children and friends and neighbors and families and estranged relations and their best friends and their friends they haven't seen in years and ex-friends and ex-lovers and adventurers and the confused and befuddled and sad and wistful and happy. We're glad you're here.

—Betsy & Mike

Everyone leaves, Brad reminded himself. No matter how many times you ask the band to run through it just one more time, or ask someone to stay one more day, or offer to go to counseling, or promise to stop drinking or to be a better listener or to "hold down the fort so you can go back to school and finish your degree," you can only really ever hope to postpone the inevitable.

Eventually, everyone leaves.

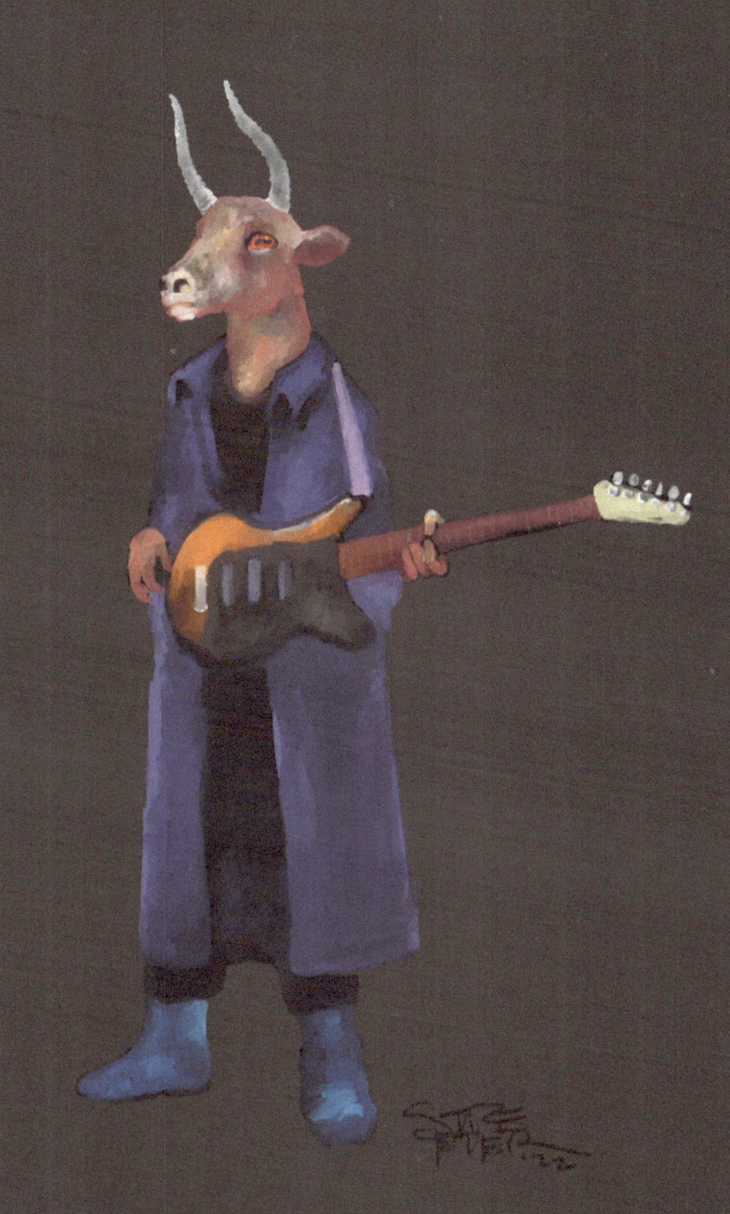

"How much time is left?"

"I'll add another ten minutes if you ask again."

"How come Bobby doesn't have corner punishment?"

"Bobby's punishment is helping your father in the yard."

"I'd rather do that than stand in the corner—"

"No more talking."

"Did Grandma and Grandpa make you stand in the corner when you did something bad?"

"No, they… "

"Mom, are you crying?"

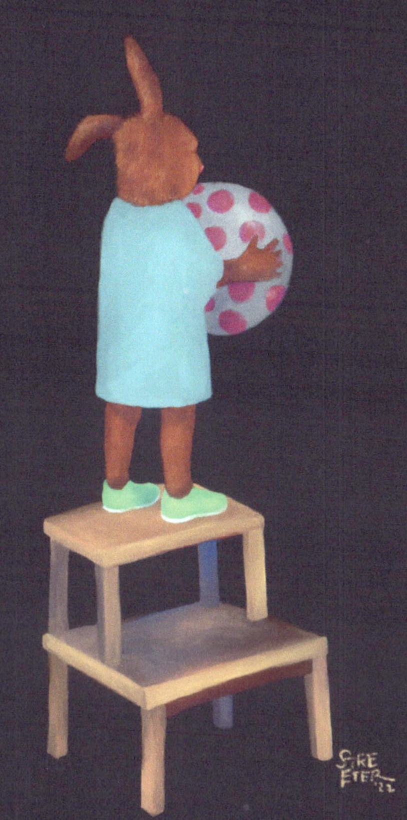

Once a year, Carlos would send his wife Maria Luisa off to a retreat. He would happily pay for her to take a friend or two along, too. *Make it a party*, he'd say. She deserved it, after all. She'd raised three kids. (The oldest was now married and expecting their first grandchild. The other two were doing well in college. Mario was thinking of medical school.) She kept the family home immaculate. She was thrust into the role of hostess whenever he had to entertain a vendor. *I wouldn't be where I am today without you, my love*, he'd say to her. And he meant it. So once a year, he did this for her. He enjoyed knowing she was being pampered.

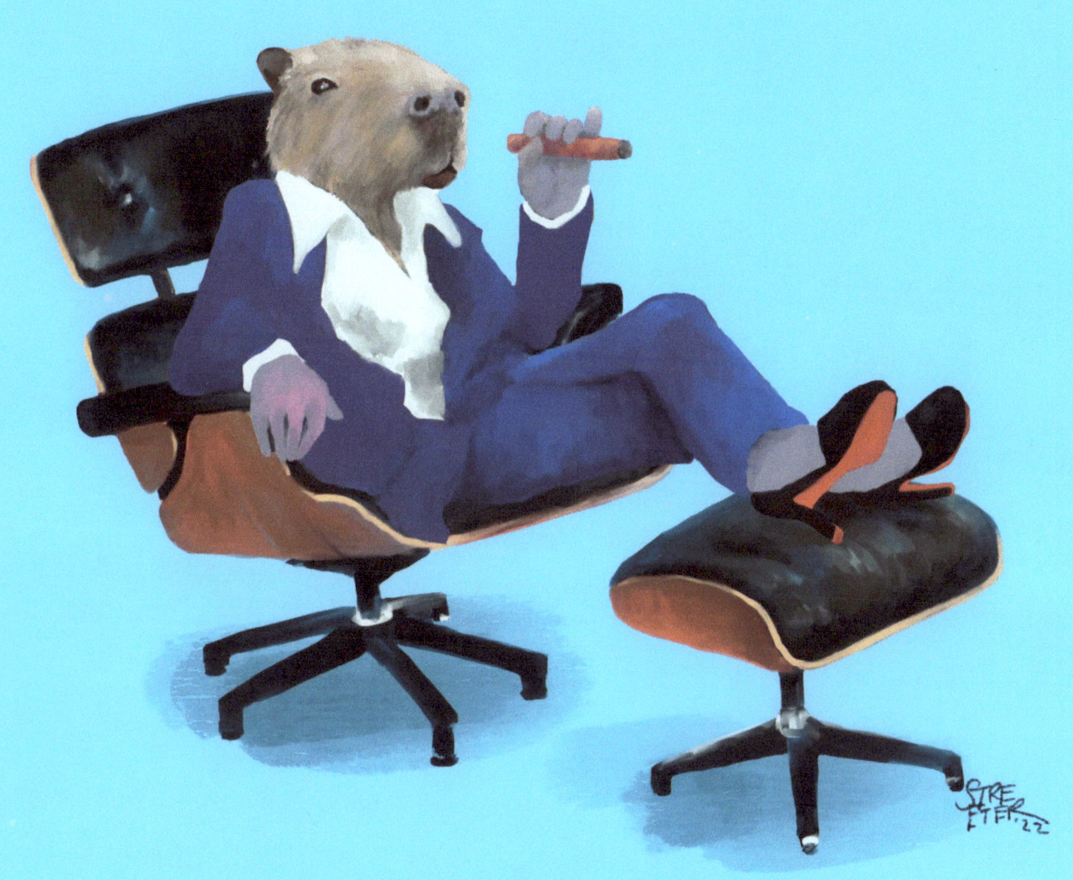

Sabrina looked across the table at this young woman she'd only met twenty minutes ago. In that short amount of time, she'd learned the following: Her name was Alice. She was 24 years old. She had a Russian Literature degree from Cal. She'd signed up for one of those online DNA services. She'd been looking for her birth mother since she was a teenager. And with every detail she added to her story, Alice's hand moved just a little bit across the table, closer to Sabrina's.

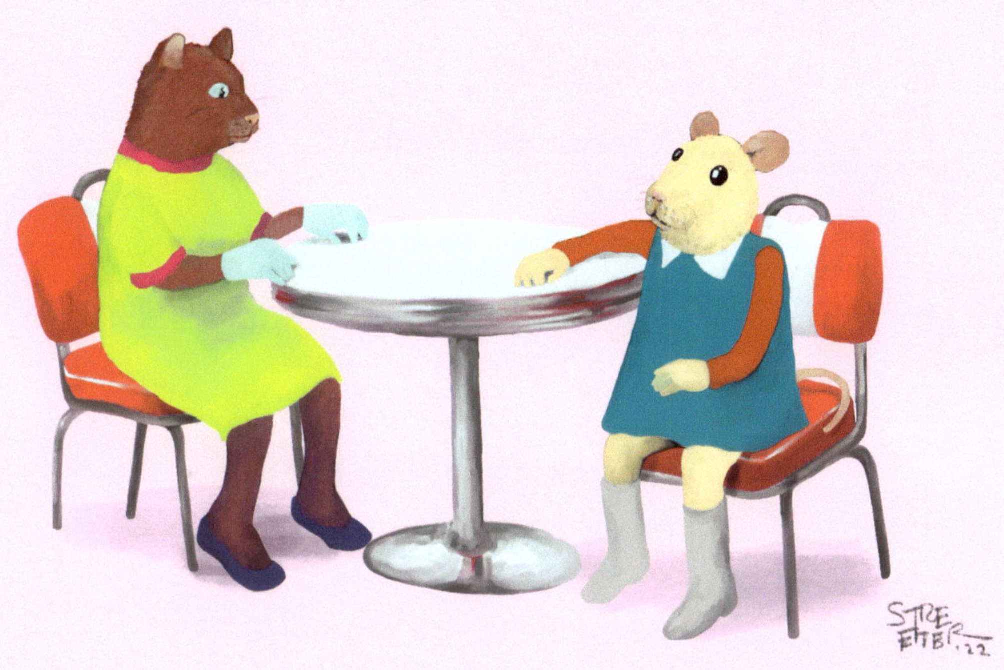

Cassidy signed up for this. He and Sheila had been married twenty-three years, and they needed a spark. So they went to counseling. Their therapist, who had some pretty out-there ideas, suggested opening up the relationship. Sheila agreed almost immediately, and Cassidy reluctantly followed. Anything for Sheila. Sheila talked to her friend Brenda, Brenda said *sure, why not*. And now they were in there, and he was out here, and they were waiting for him, but he wasn't ready.

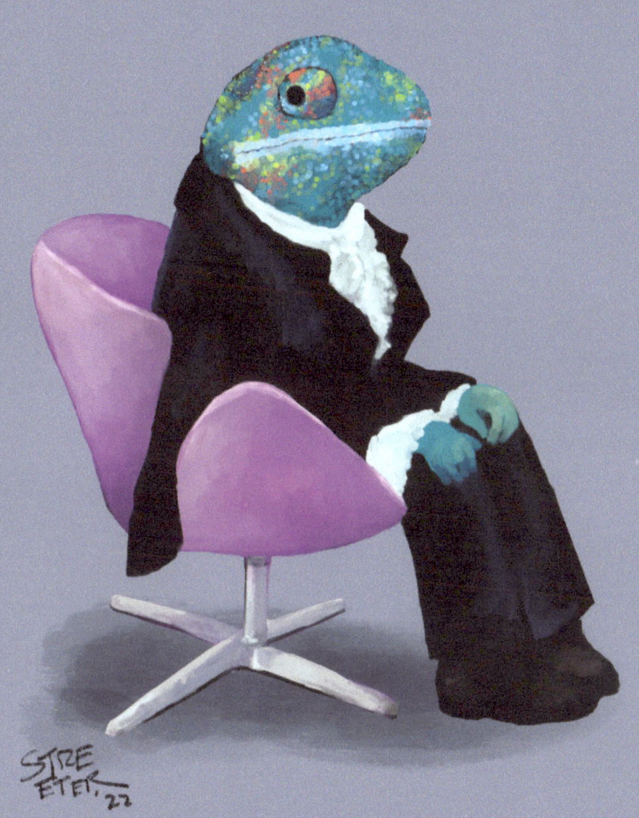
STRE
ETER. '22

Zack waited in the bowling alley, as they'd agreed. He didn't order anything, and luckily the staff was leaving him alone. His job was easy. All he had to do was wait. At this moment, Joyce was telling her husband their marriage was over. Then she'd grab her bag from the closet, packed ahead of time, as they'd agreed. She'd toss it in the car, and they'd meet here in the bowling alley across town.

This all took time, Zack reminded himself, as he settled into his third hour of waiting.

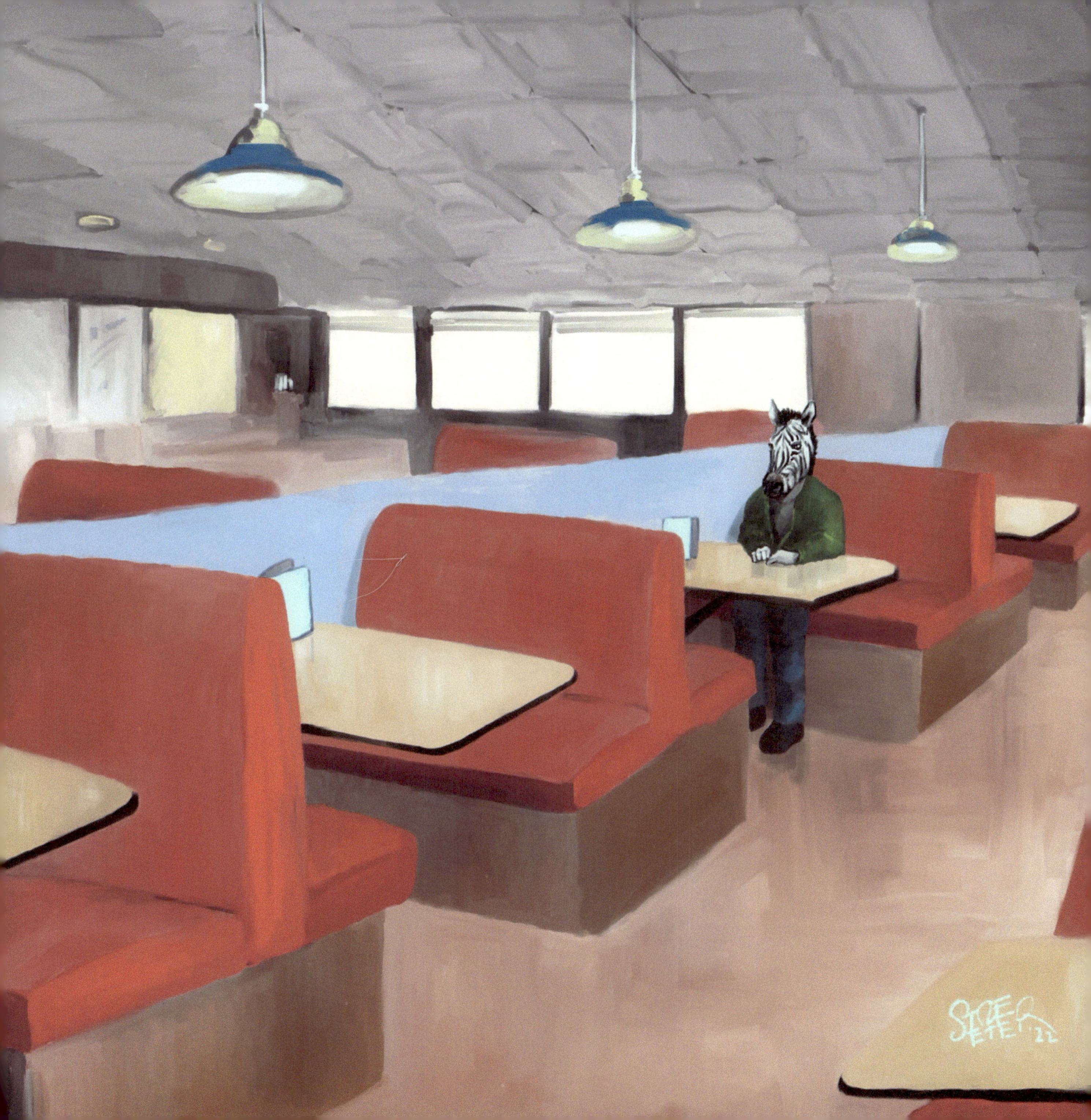

For twenty-two years, Claude has been coming to his desk at the Department of Marriage Licenses inside City Hall. For twenty-two years he showed up promptly at 9:00 a.m., issued licenses to happy couples until half-past noon, then took his lunch in the small alcove right outside his office. For the first twenty-one years of Claude's time at the Department of Marriage Licenses at City Hall, lunch was a tuna sandwich that his wife Syd had packed for him. For the last year, Claude has been trying to recreate that tuna sandwich.

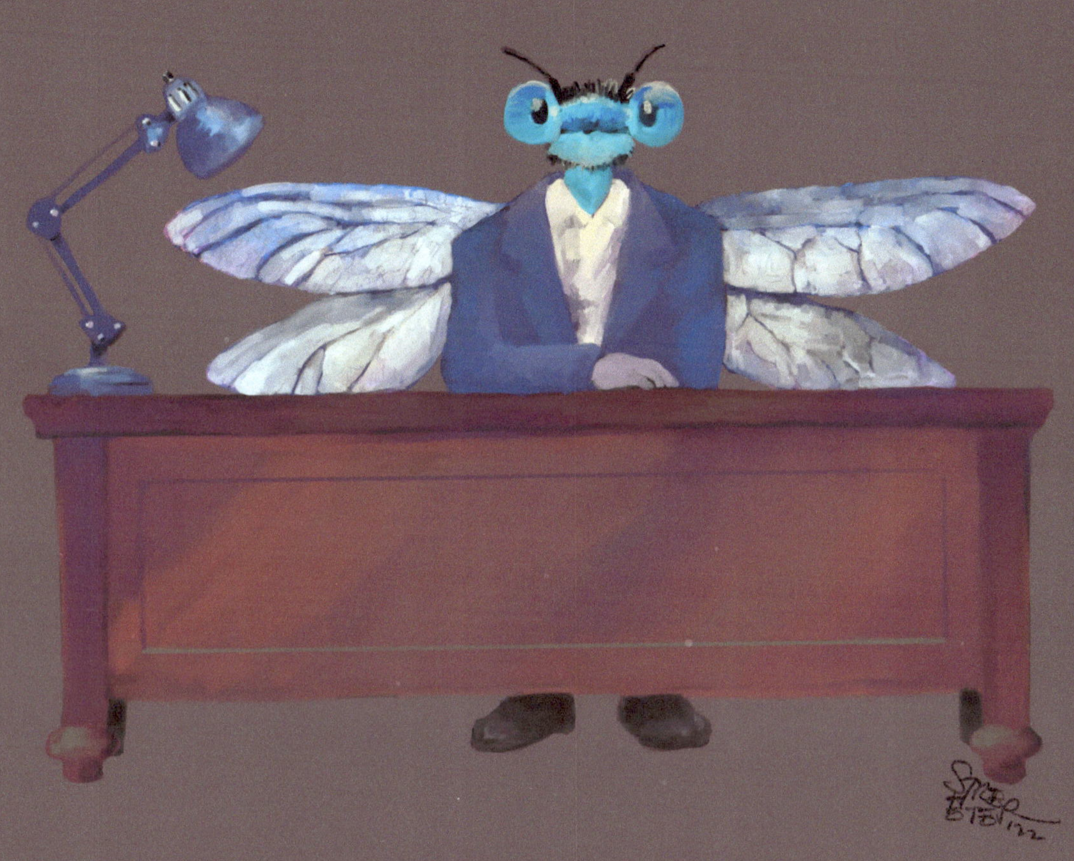

Cecil waited. Cecil waited because any moment now his phone would ring, and he'd see his wife's name, he'd pick it up, and she'd say she was sorry. And he'd walk back a few things that he said as well. There'd be uncomfortable moments of silence, sure, and possibly even a couple of moments where everything would threaten to unravel. But they'd eventually talk through it. And eventually one of them would say, "Hey, it's kinda silly that we're doing this on the phone." And he'd uncork a bottle of wine and wait for her to come through the door. Cecil waited. Every day he waited. Any moment now his phone would ring.

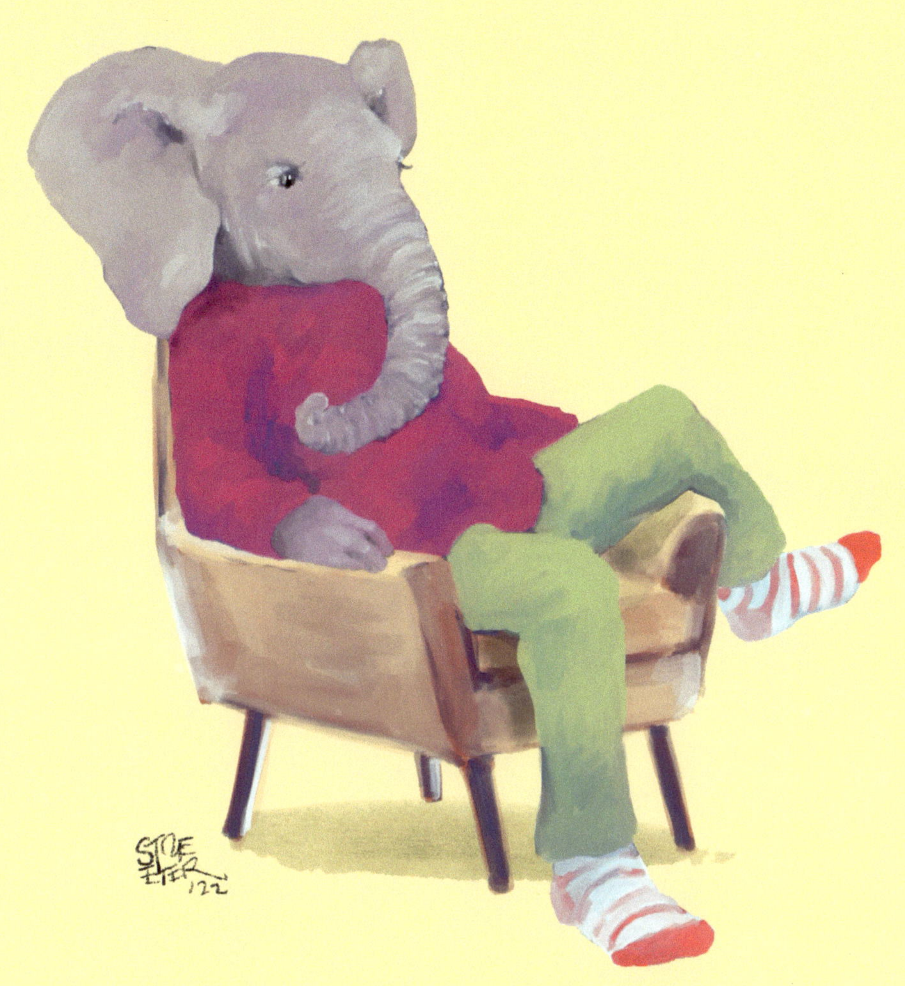

"Oh boy, oh boy," thought Felix. "You've done it now." Sure, he'd always found Sabrina charming and incredibly cute, but she was with Max. The two of them had been going out for almost a year. And the three of them went out drinking almost every week, so tonight was just a typical night. Until they all jumped into a cab, Sabrina sitting next to him, their legs making contact, and Felix, using a bumpy road as an excuse, locked pinkies with her. She didn't recoil. And as she and Max got out of the cab, she squeezed his paw just a little and said, "We'll see you next week, sweetie."

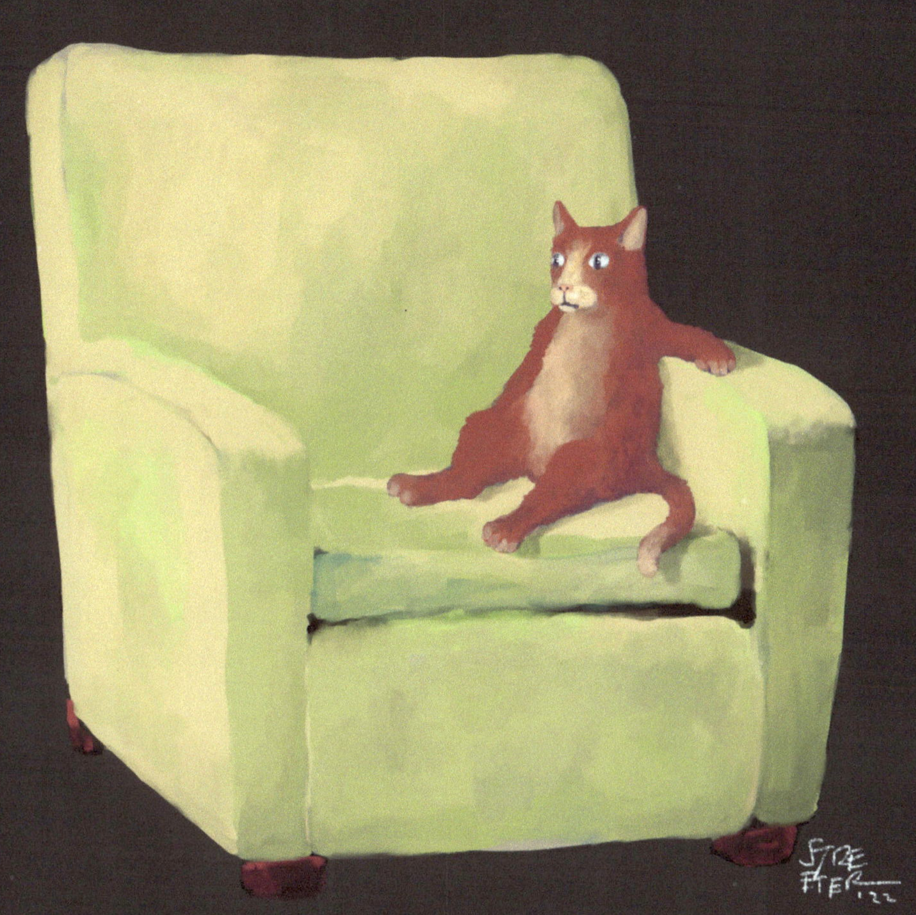

Chris rearranged the chairs in their new office for the third time. It was important that the couple were facing each other but also able to talk to Chris directly. Like a perfect triangle. Except with Chris a little further back, with their fresh diploma hanging casually behind them. And the couple's chairs had to be close, not too close, but still close. After all, they were the patients, and Chris was just here to help. The same way Chris had tried to help their own parents.

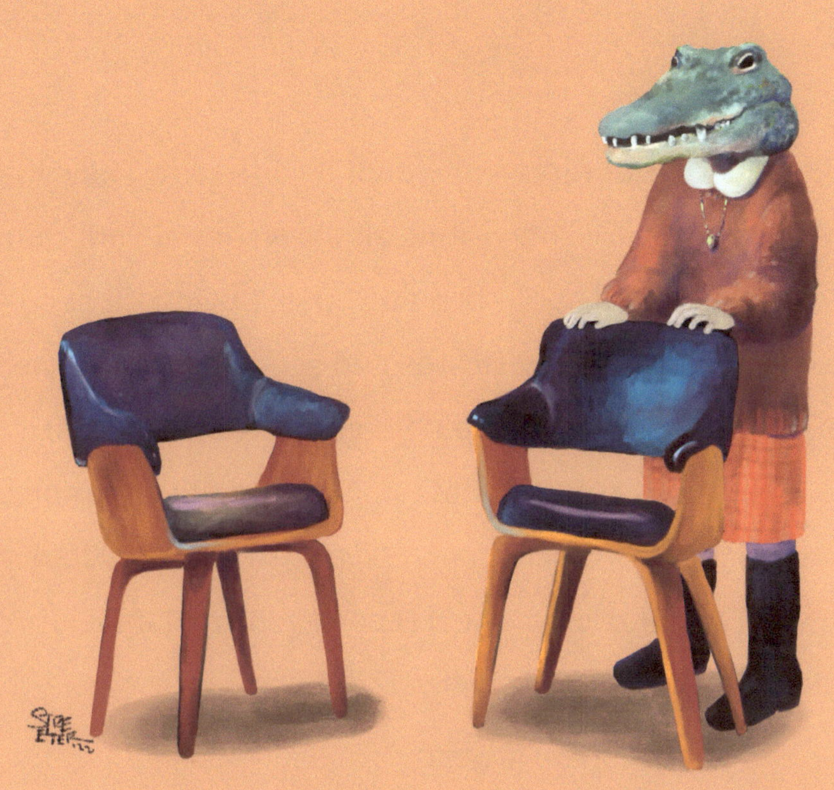

Geoffrey thought retirement would be different. They'd talked about buying an RV and visiting all the National Parks. She was mostly excited about the gift shops. Buying those silly "wish you were here" postcards and sending them to the kids, who'd long ago dispersed to different states to start their own lives. They'd buy souvenir hats, commemorative thimbles, spoons, and pens. *You're gonna fill the RV with souvenirs*, he told her. *That's the plan*, she'd reply, as she'd plant a kiss on his lips and wander off to make more plans.

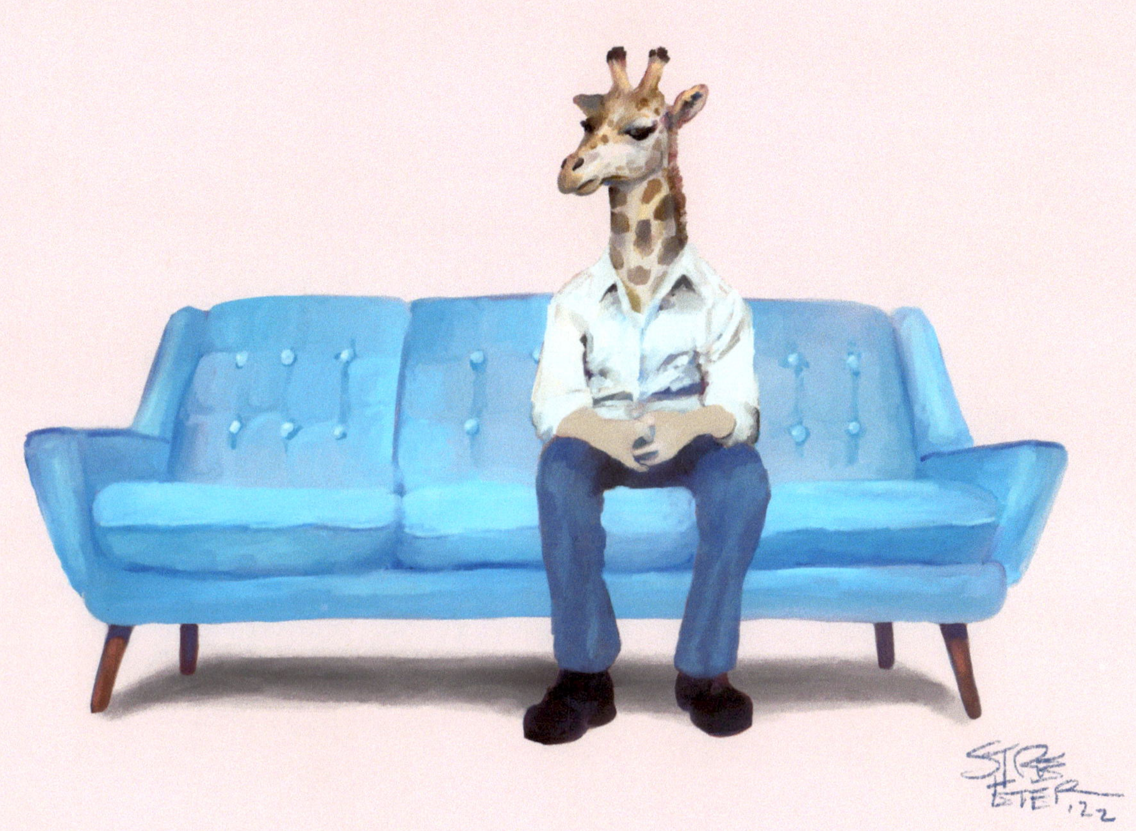

Reggie always looked forward to his sessions with Dr. Bill. It was nice to have an adult listen to him. He especially liked it when Dr. Bill asked follow-up questions, like he was following along. He even remembered the names of all of Reggie's friends, which admittedly wasn't too hard because there were only three. And Brad came up the most. In fact, Brad was the reason Reggie's parents first brought him to Dr. Bill. But the best part was when they were done talking and Reggie got to pick a candy bar out of the big bowl. He usually got a Twix and shared it with Brad the next day.

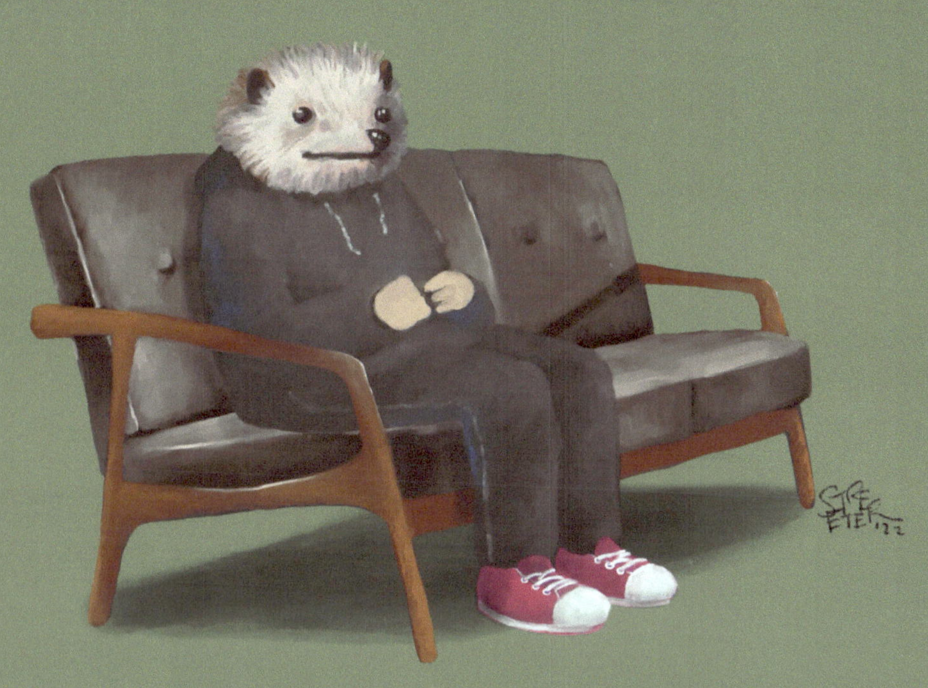

Beatrice was beginning to worry. She'd set the table over an hour ago, and even with a cover on the casserole dish, it wasn't going to stay warm forever. It wasn't like Omar to come home late. And with the sun setting earlier at this time of year she worried about him driving in the dark. His eyesight wasn't what it used to be. *Any minute now he'll walk through that door*, she told herself. Maybe she should reheat the casserole.

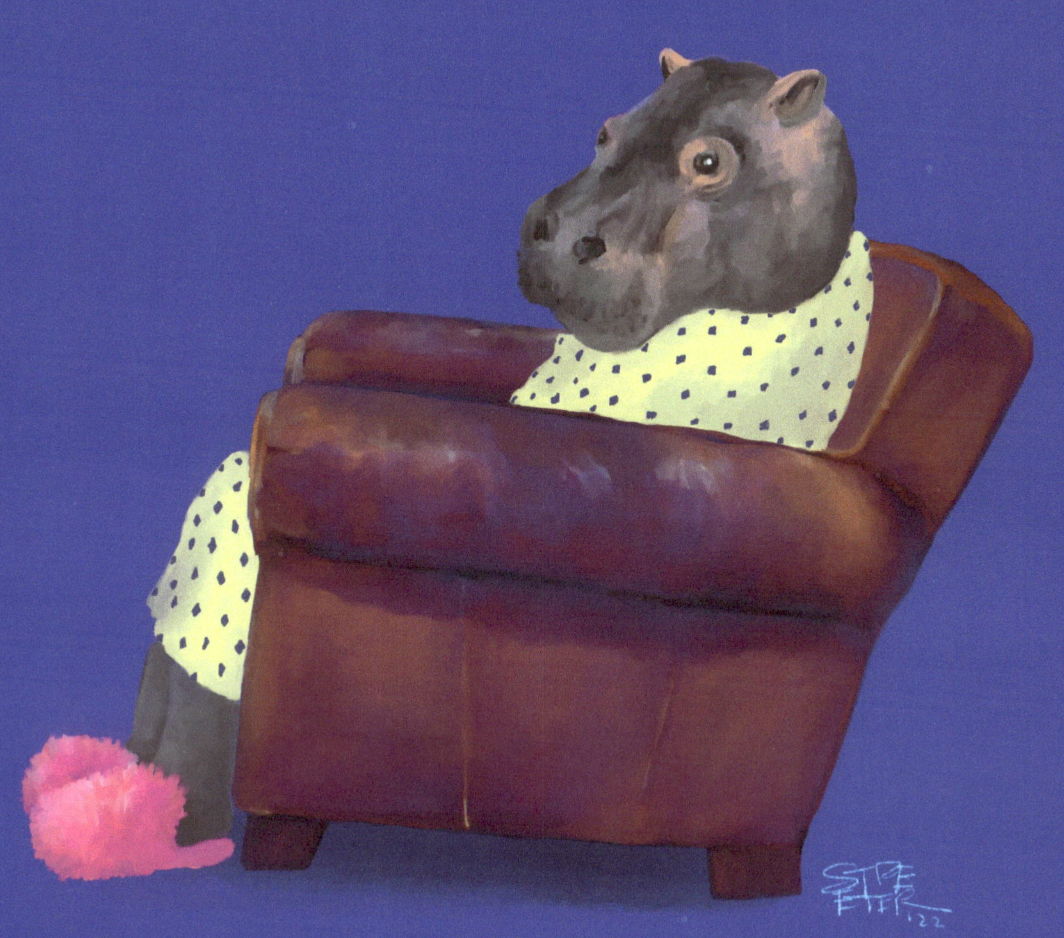

He goes to dress stores sometimes, sits on a couch, and watches women picking out outfits, walking in and out of the dressing room. He's not being creepy. Their movements remind him of his wife. And for a few brief minutes he pictures her selecting a top, turning to him, sitting on that same couch years earlier, and gauging his reaction.

He slowly gets up, tips his hat to the guard by the door, and walks towards where the automat used to be.

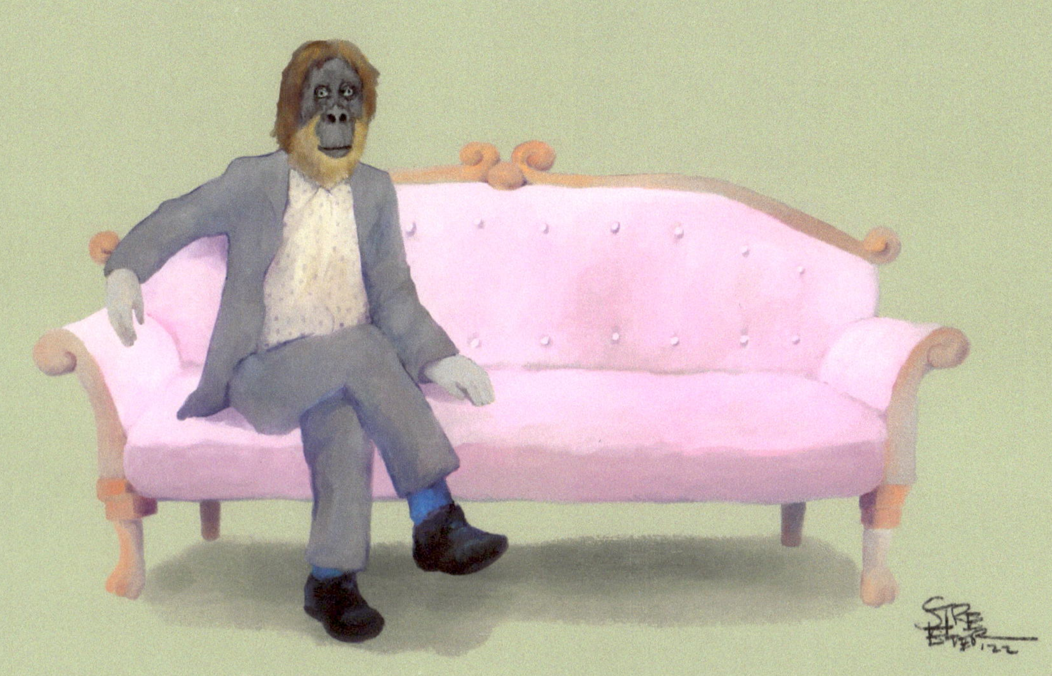

Rae was a confident woman at the height of her sexual peak. She was committed to pushing the envelope of sexual exploration while maintaining boundaries of consent, safety, and good health. She enjoyed looking after her partners, and expected the same of them. She knew her limits, discussed them ahead of time, and made explicit agreements. Brad knew “nevermore” wasn’t the safe word. Brad knew what that did to her. And yet, Rae was about to have this conversation with her therapist one more time.

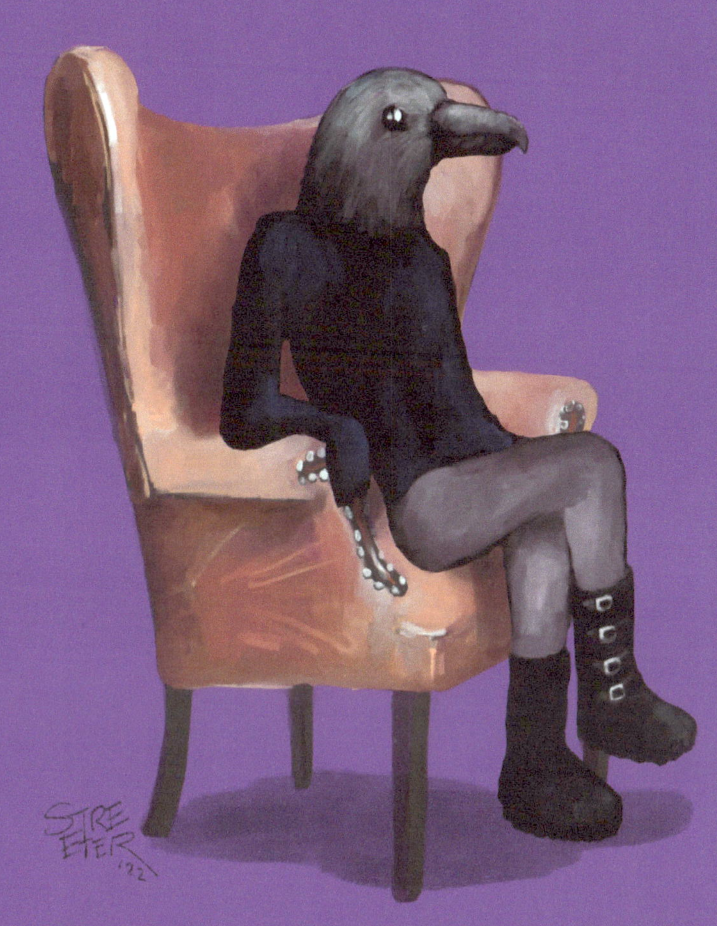
STREETER '22

Gene's first bachelor party was in his best man Eli's backyard. Everyone was broke. Eli invited a bunch of guys from work, and Mabel, who was like one of the guys, and they each brought a six-pack. Eli fucked Mabel in the backyard shed. Gene's second bachelor party was in a suite at the Ritz. Eli, again the best man, invited the fellas from the firm, and provided strippers, cigars, and a mountain of cocaine. Tonight, back in his room after his third bachelor party, Gene wondered if he was maybe getting too old for this. But mostly he missed Eli.

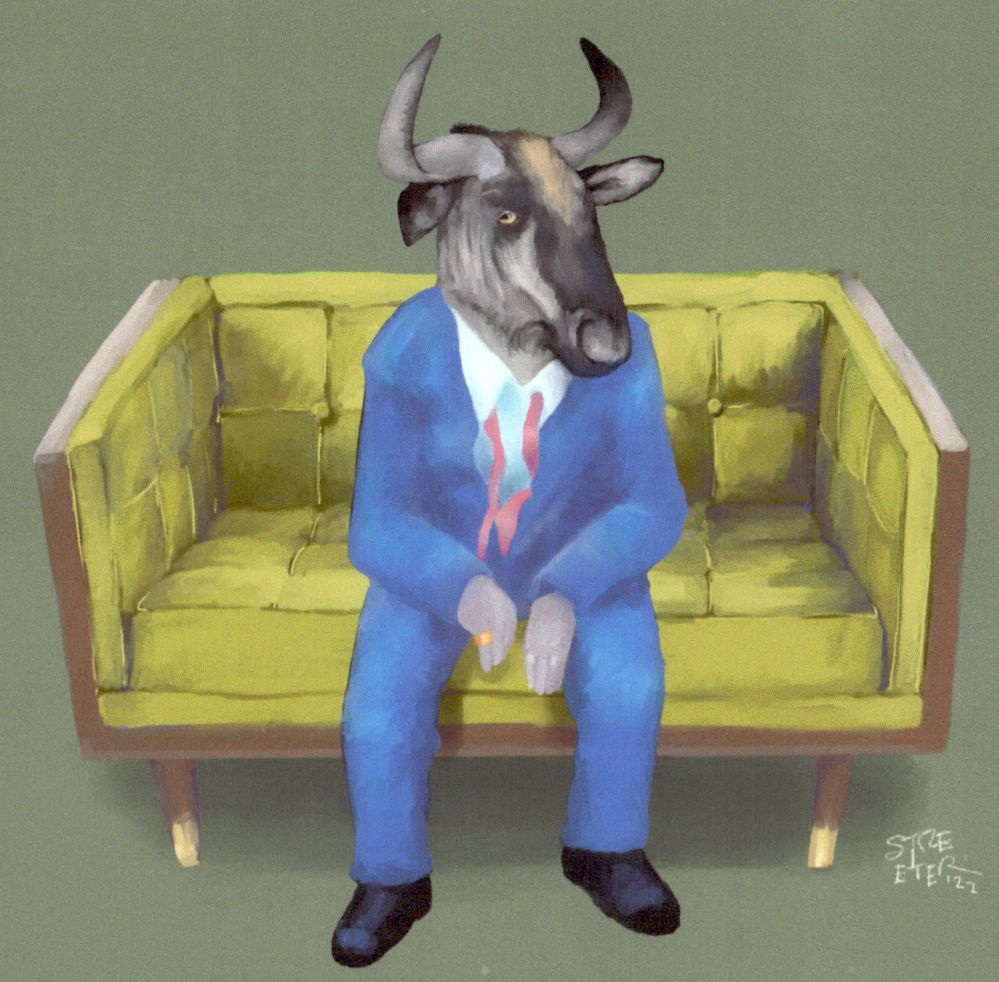

Trevor had been in marketing for over twenty years, if you counted his first job in the mailroom, which—while not *technically* a marketing job—was at a marketing firm. He learned as much as he could while pushing the little mail cart around the office. He'd deliver to copywriters. He'd deliver to illustrators. He'd deliver to sales. And he kept his ears and eyes open. When an intern job opened up, he pounced. He achieved everything on hustle and merit. And now that his father was stepping down, he was finally getting a chance at running the whole enchilada.

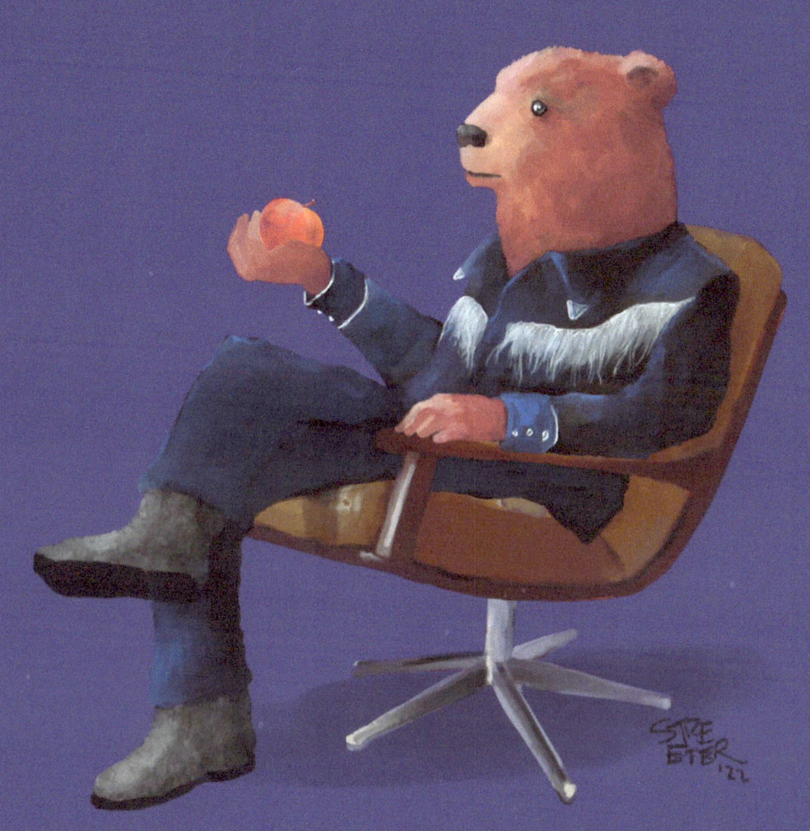

Selena was looking forward to dinner. Her whole life she'd lived in her sister's shadow. *Why can't you get good grades like Debra?* her mother would ask. *We're going to need more shelf space for Debra's trophies*, her father would say. But tonight, three days shy of her fifteenth birthday, Selena would announce to her parents that she was growing life inside her.

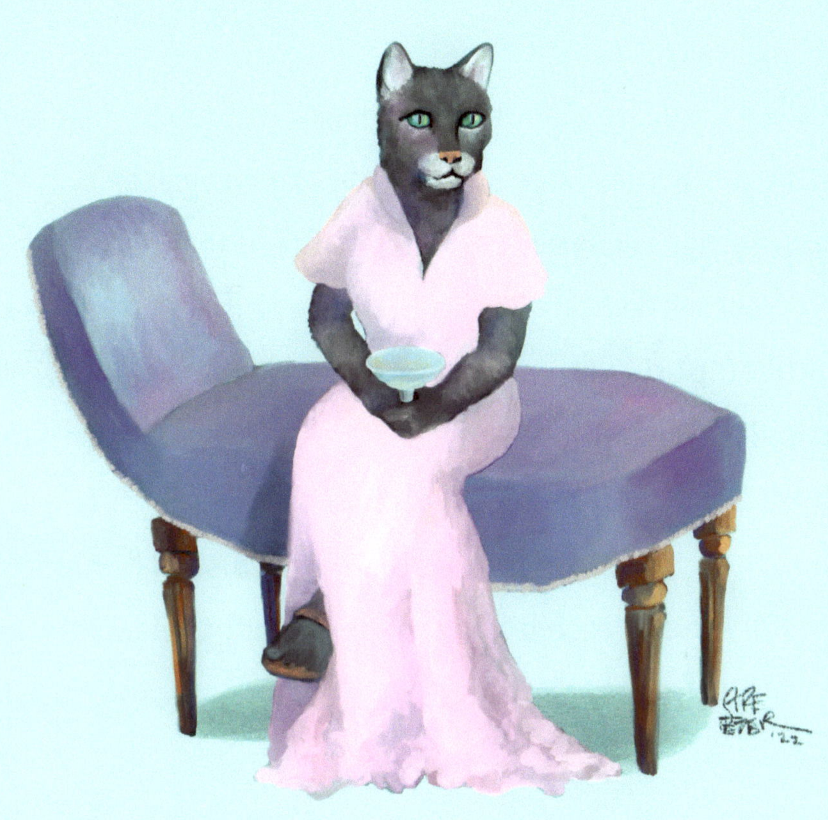

Natalie called her grandmother every Sunday at exactly 12:15 p.m. By then, mass was well underway. Her grandmother always went at noon. She'd leave a message with exactly one non-intimate detail about her week, a short weather report, a mention of how much she missed a particular dish her grandmother made (there were many to choose from), and ask how Grandpa was doing. She'd end by telling her grandmother how much she missed her, and that hopefully she'd catch her next week. Except this week her dad answered and said, "Natalie, sweetie, I have some bad news."

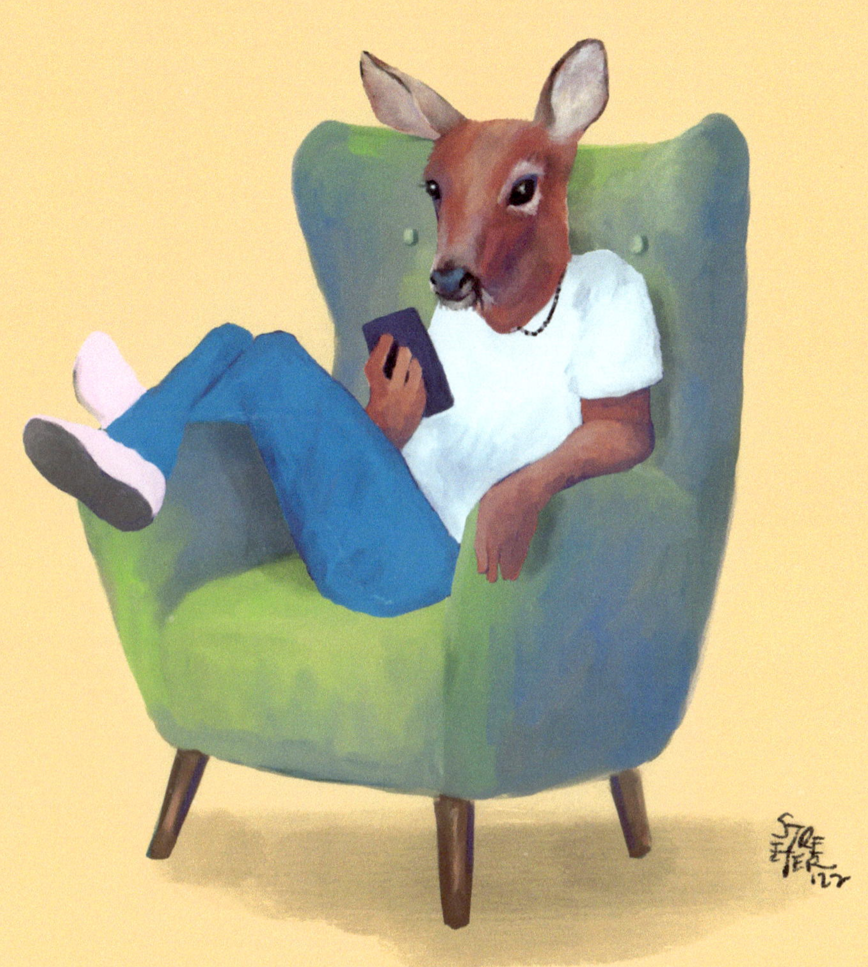

As long as Freida could remember, Saturday afternoons included a walk to the soda fountain with Dad. She'd spend the morning watching cartoons, and then eventually Dad would wake up. He'd pat her on the head, call her Sport, and half-heartedly tell her she was sitting too close to the TV. She'd half-heartedly scoot back. He'd make her a peanut butter and jelly sandwich and head off to the garage to work on the Dart. After a few hours, he'd walk back in the house covered in oil and grease. He'd shower, put on a clean t-shirt, grab his hat, and say, "C'mon, Sport."

They always sat at the counter. He'd have coffee, sometimes pie, and she'd have a sundae. She still went every Saturday. She still ordered her sundae, hardly ever putting much of a dent in it anymore. Then she'd order a small coffee to go, walk the four blocks to the cemetery, and leave it on his headstone.

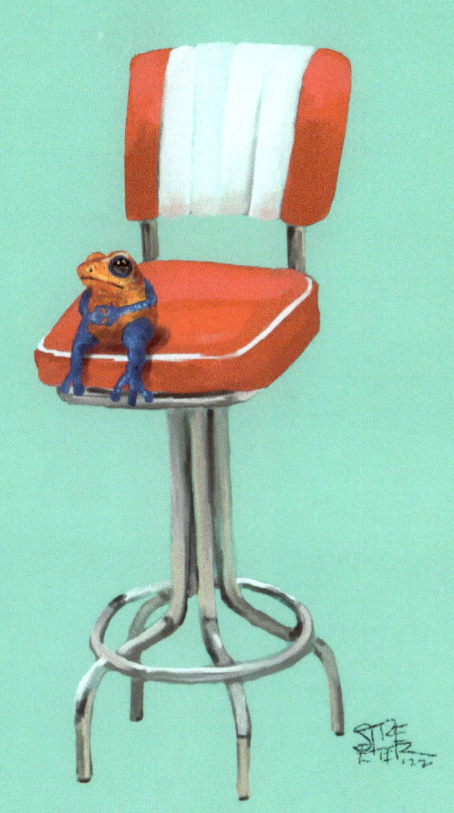

Everything changed in an instant. Of course, Walter knew there would be pain. He'd even considered that some of it might be his. But he thought most of that pain would be something he'd unfairly have to endure. *Other people's feelings*, he thought. *Other people's needs*. *Other people's reliance on him.* Mostly Walter thought of his freedom. A life unencumbered by responsibility. A life without shackles. A life where he could gallop at full speed, free of the yoke of family. But right now, in this instant, with his bag packed, and the car in the driveway already facing the street, Walter realized he was going to miss at least half of his son's life.

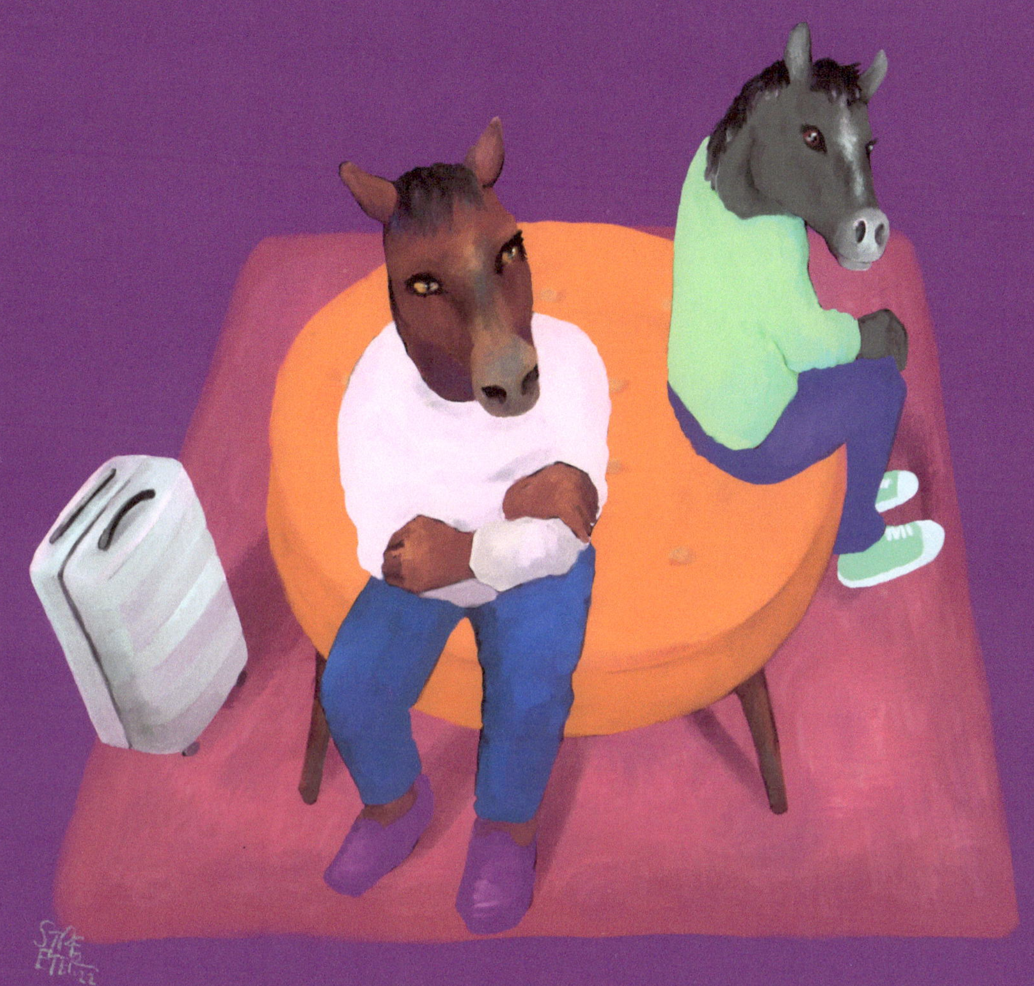

Pablo hadn't seen his father in years. Any minute now, a cab was going to pull up outside his house, and his father would emerge from it. He'd make his way up the walk and knock on the door. Pablo would walk to the door and… He'd gone over this moment so many times. He'd gone over all the variables. He'd anticipated every outcome he could think of. He'd discussed them all with his therapist. She was the one who came up with the flamenco number. His father wouldn't be expecting that. Pablo would have the element of surprise in his corner. And yet, Pablo kept running one scenario through his mind: he could open the door, and his father would say, *I've missed you, son.*

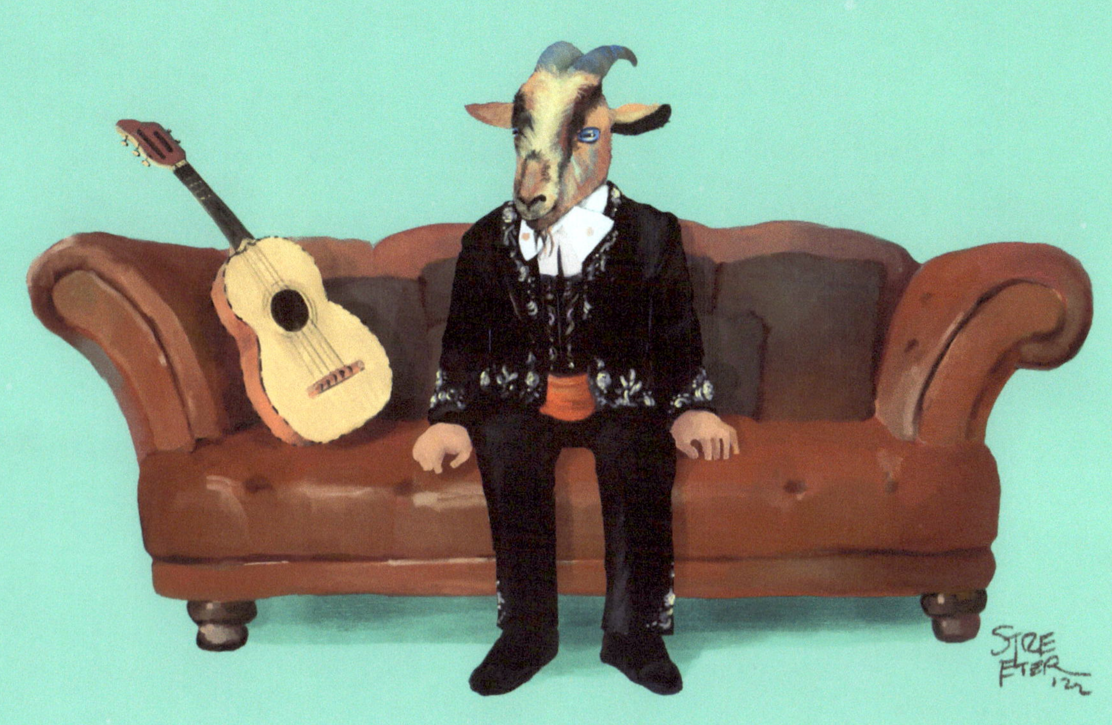

Liz spent thirty-three years in the public school system. First, as a teacher's aide for a couple of years; then a substitute social studies and English teacher traveling all over the district for a few years; then settling in as a 7th grade English teacher at McKinley Junior High for a decade; and finally Assistant Principal at the same place until her retirement last year. Along the way, she'd gone from a nervous, tentative, dare-she-say even *scared* teaching college grad to a confident, mature woman who could de-escalate the rowdiest of situations with both students and parents. And yet, sitting here, at age 65, ready to introduce herself to her siblings as Liz, was the first time she understood what it was like to feel fierce.

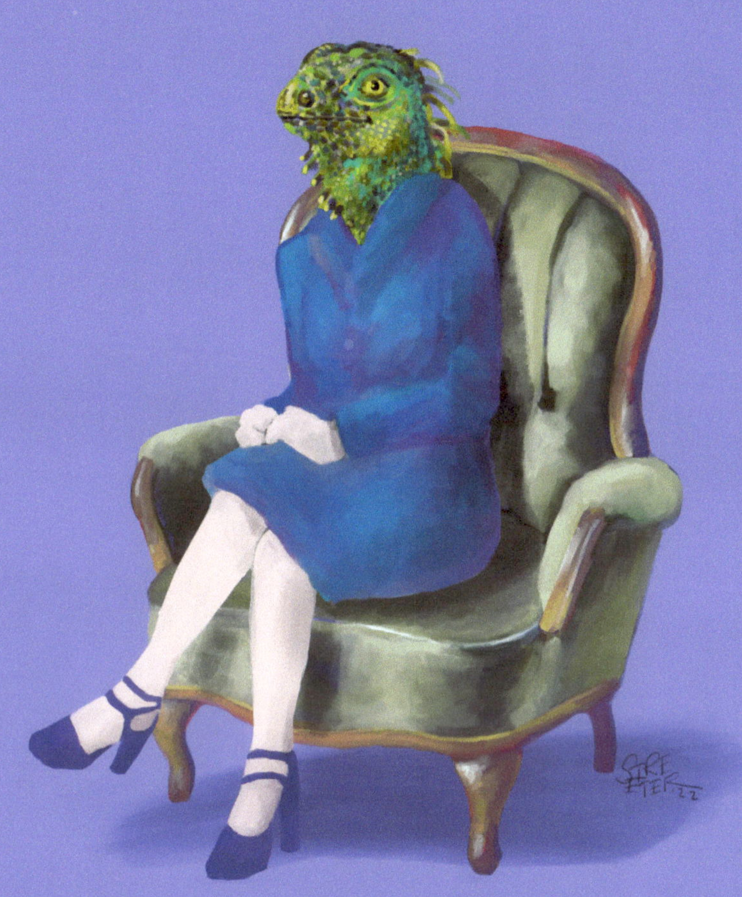

Stephen hated gym class. Well, I guess it wasn't gym class specifically that he hated, it was the shower room after gym class. Well, it wasn't so much that he hated the shower room, but that he felt like he looked forward to it for all the wrong reasons. How could something that was supposed to get you clean make you feel so dirty?

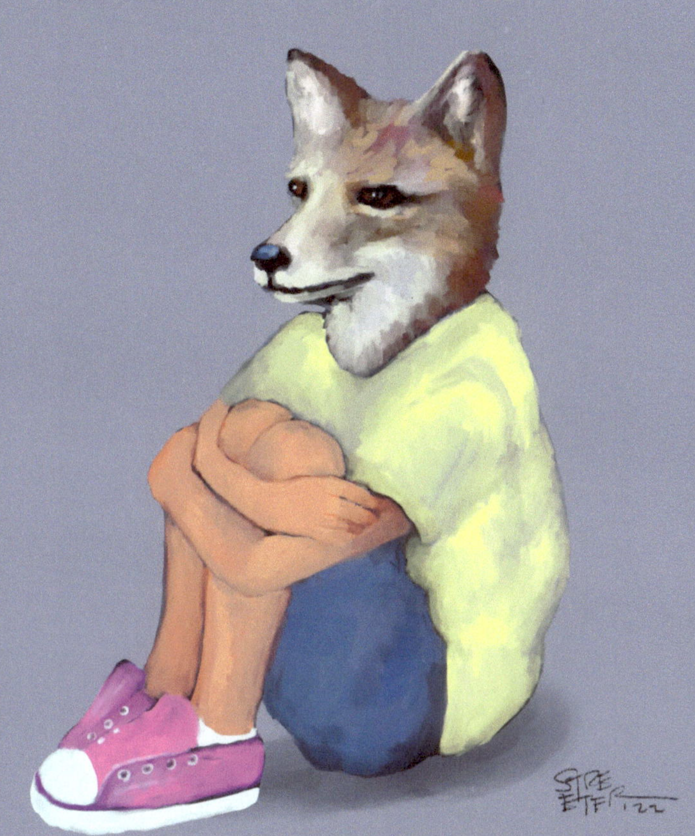

Once again, Dr. Ogilvy was taking Chad's side and Duke was sick of it. Tumblers need to be loaded in the dishwasher upside-down, otherwise they fill with water. What does compassion or empathy have to do with it? There is right, and there is wrong! Was Duke supposed to just let the world grow stupid around him in search of happiness? No, Duke would rather be right than happy.

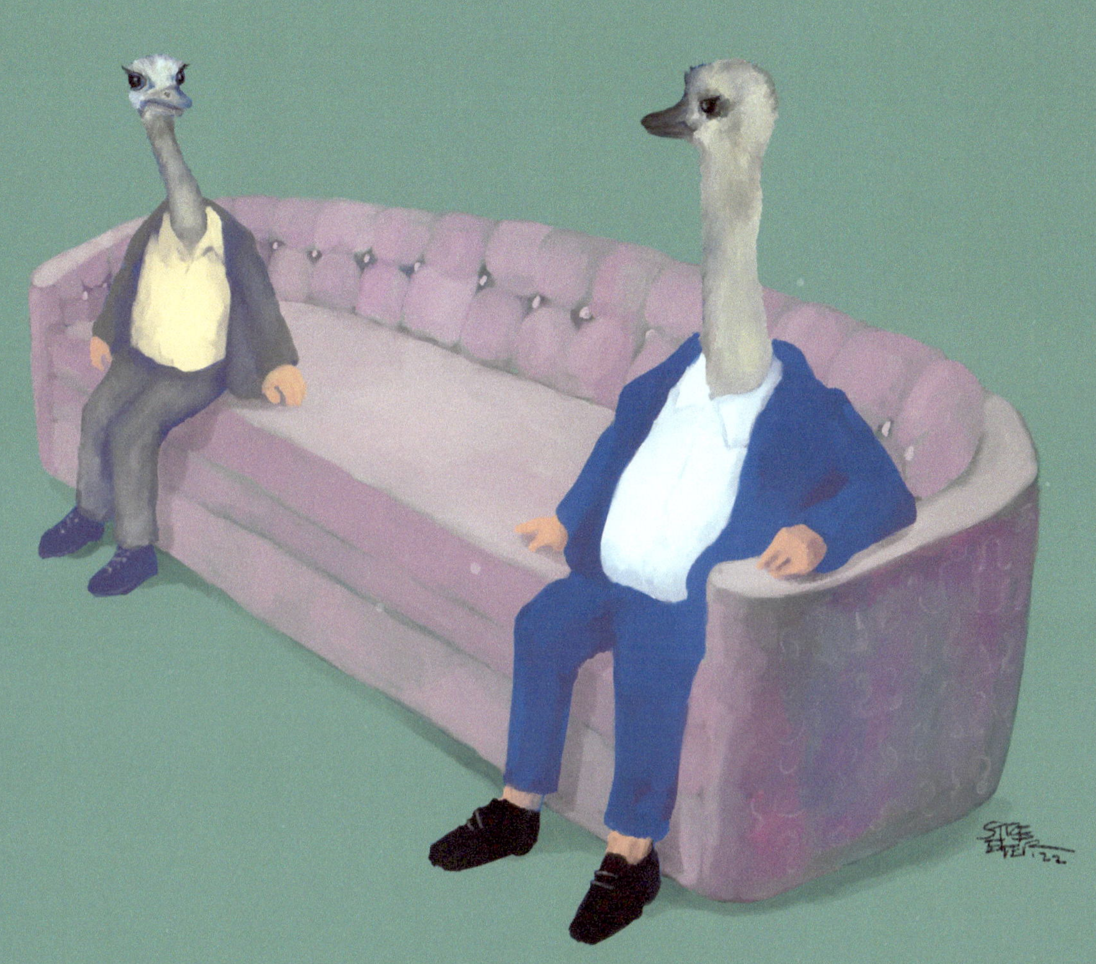

Yes, the election had been close, but if he made that “beaten by a hare” joke one more time she was going to shove that microphone up his ass.

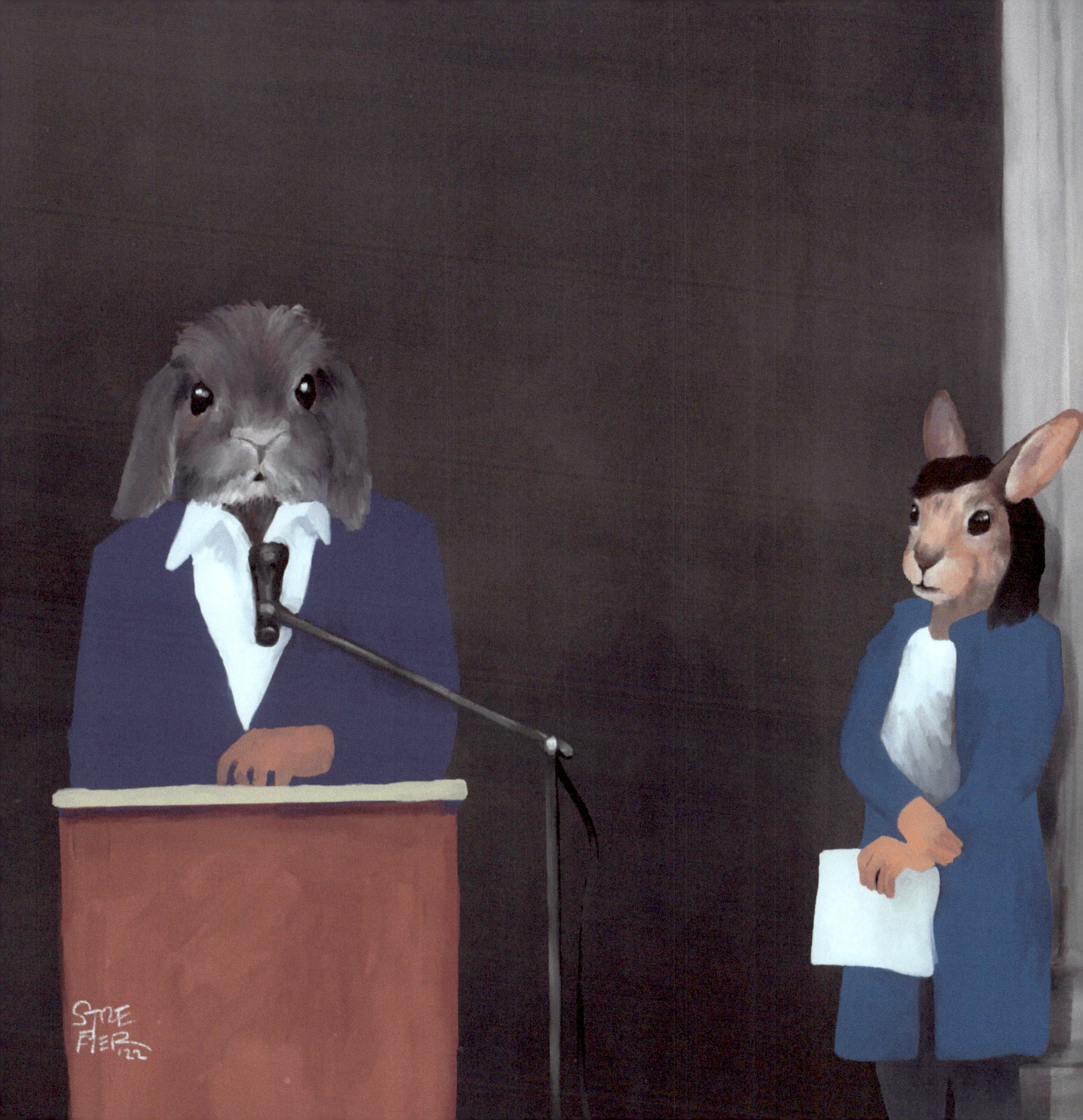

The salesgirl assured Kevin that he was a hat person. He wanted to believe her, so he did. He bought the hat. He woke up the next morning excited for the first Zoom call of the day. “I’m going to wear my hat!” he said to no one in particular in his studio apartment. He showered, brushed his teeth, poured himself a cup of coffee and sat down in front of his laptop. Before joining the Zoom he picked up his hat from next to the laptop and adjusted it in the mirror to his right. He connected with the 20 other people on the call. “Kevin, what the fuck is on your head?!” said Martha.

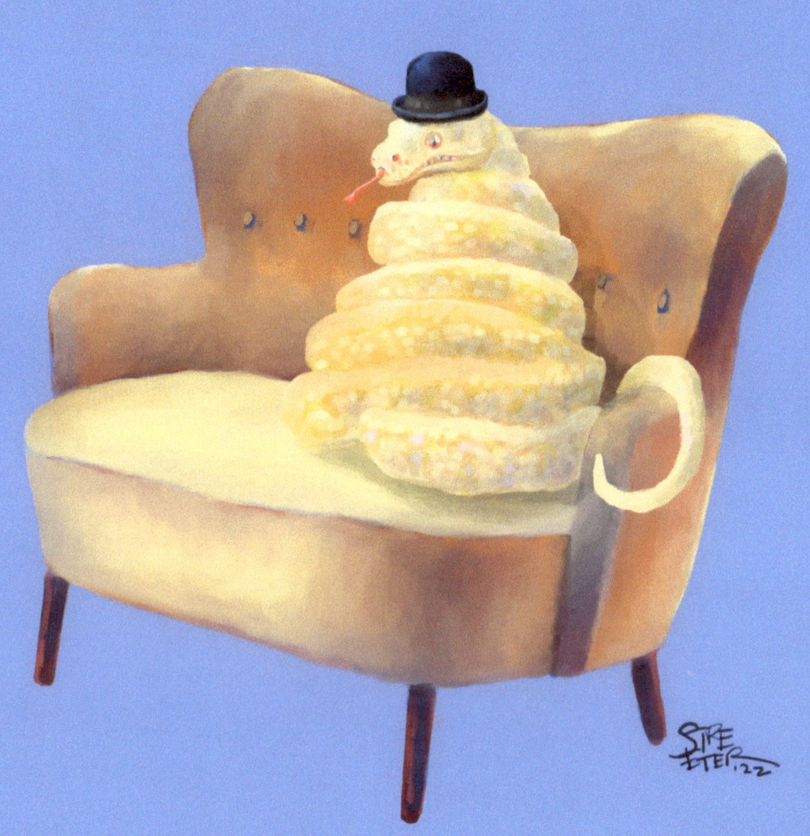

Once a year, Rocky put on his red dancing boots and reminisced about going out until dawn. Dancing. Drinking. Popping pills. Doing lines in the bathroom with guys he'd just met on the dance floor, covered in sweat and glitter, their coke up his nose quickly followed by their tongues up his beak. He was a sight to behold back then. You could time the sunrise by Rocky walking up the hill, chest out, shirt half off, red boots cradled under one arm.

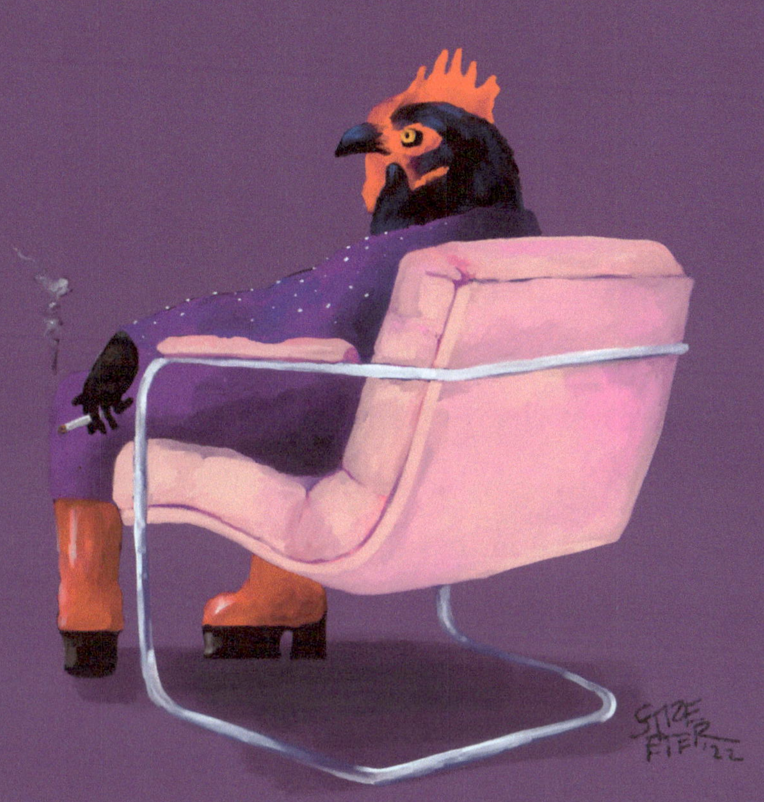

“This was the first record I ever bought,” Tony told the record store clerk. He was hoping to start a conversation, and possibly even be commended for his good taste, but she just nodded, nonplussed. “It’ll be nice to listen to it again,” he continued, as she rung him up. “The first time I bought it I paid $7.98, that’s what records cost back then.” Again, nothing. Polite professionalism as she handed him back his credit card along with a receipt before looking for the next person in line and shouting, “NEXT!”

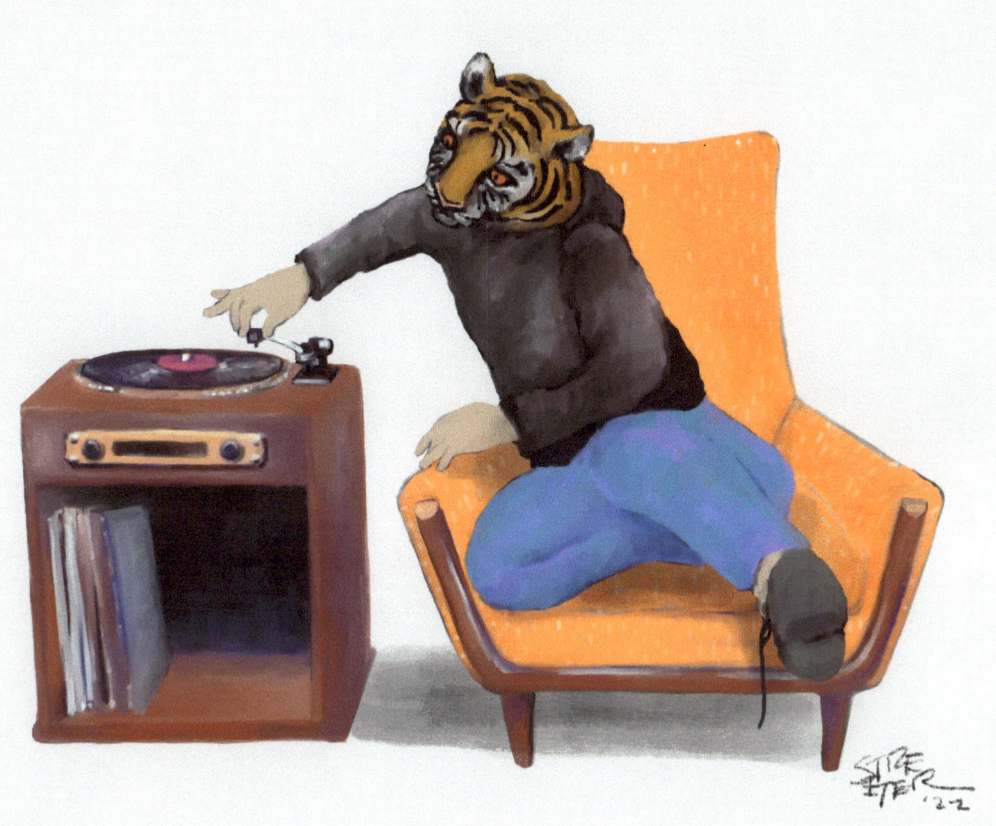

Hazel and Harriet hated adult parties. Their mother was the only one who ever brought her kids, so there were no other kids to talk to. In fact, Hazel and Harriet were pretty sure you were specifically not supposed to bring your kids to these kinds of parties. But she did, and no one stopped her because, well, they very much wanted her at these kinds of parties. So Hazel and Harriet would sit on the sofa. Waiting. Trying to take up as little space as possible. Sometimes gentlemen would walk by and tousle their hair. Sometimes a hostess would bring them plates, usually cheese, crackers, and very tiny sour pickles. Their mom would wander by from time to time to check on them. And when she gathered them to go home, they'd almost always stop at the diner for pie, or sometimes breakfast.

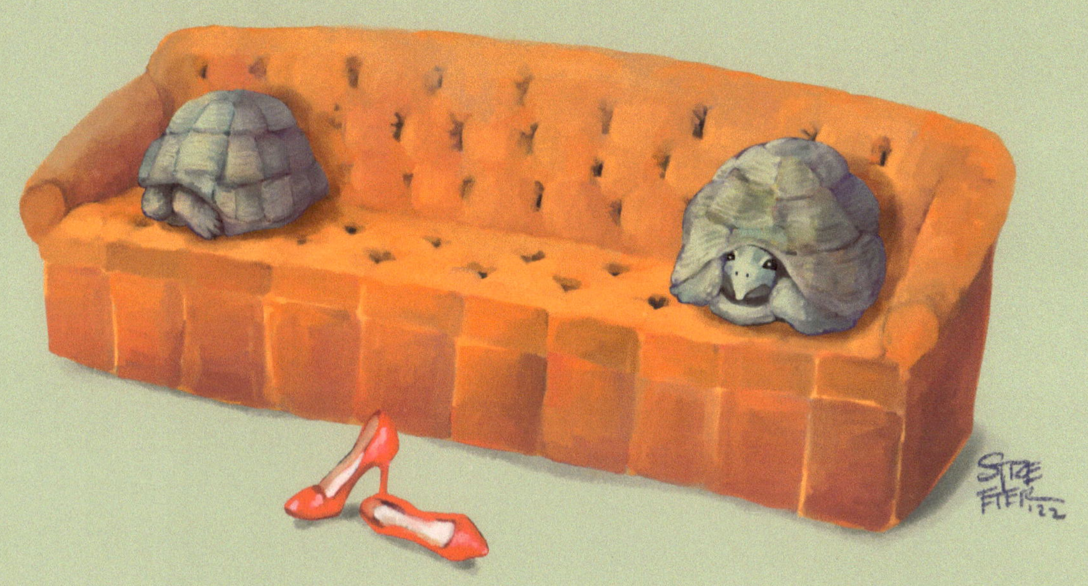

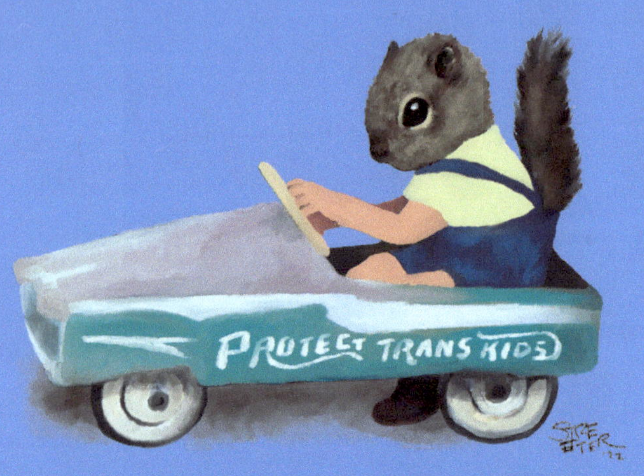
PROTECT TRANS KIDS

Betsy Streeter is an artist and native of the San Francisco East Bay. She believes that life and love are not transactions. She'd like to thank her husband Rob, her kids Jen and Sean, her parents, and her brother Richard. And Mike, for writing that first little wistful story, and then another and another, which brought this whole project to life.

Mike Monteiro is a designer, writer, and artist living in San Francisco. He believes that love is love and that trans kids should be protected and celebrated. He'd like to thank his wife Erika, his daughter Chelsea, and his dog Rupert. He'd also like to thank Betsy Streeter for trusting him to tell the stories of her amazing characters.

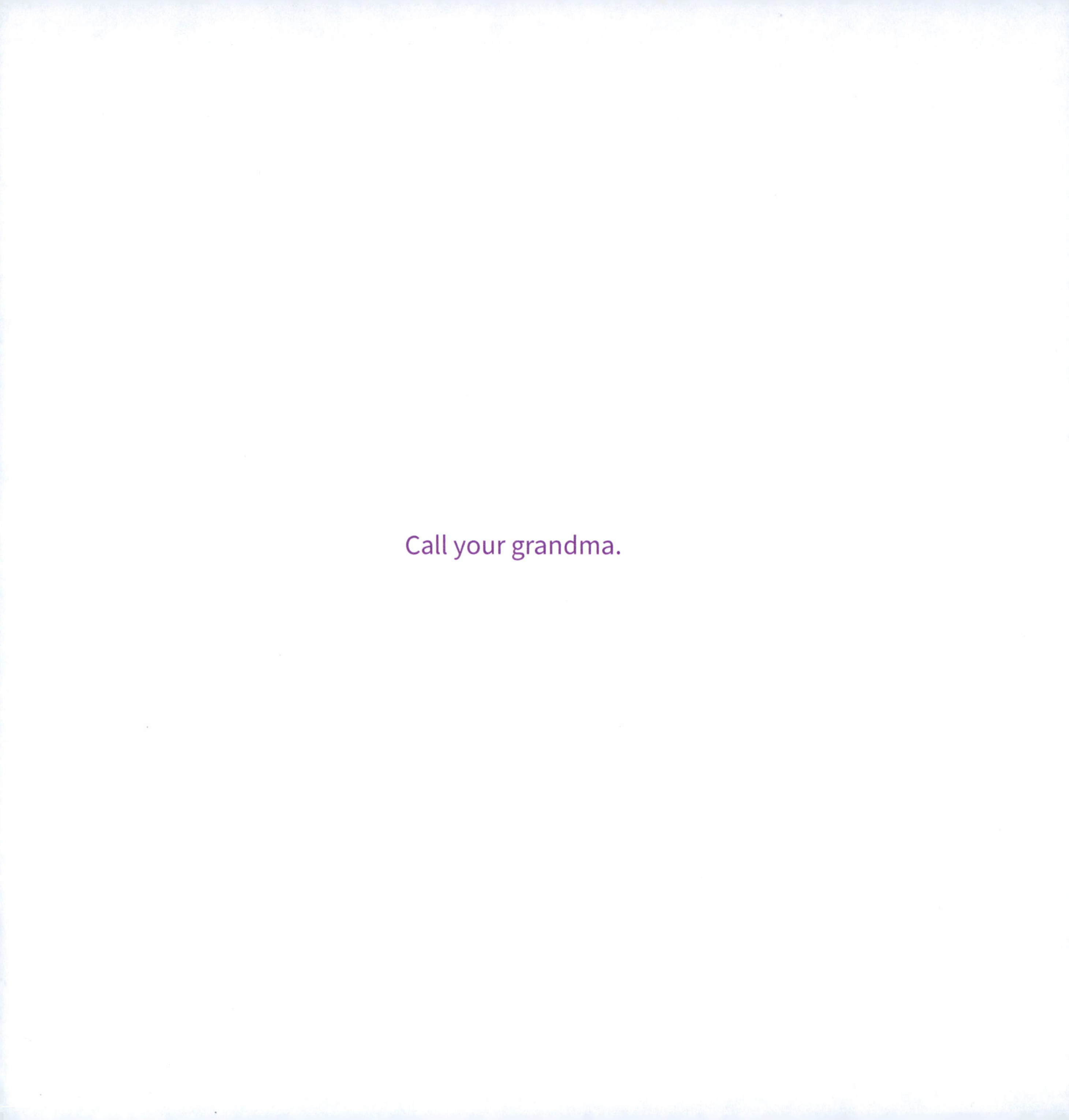

Call your grandma.

CPSIA information can be obtained
at www.ICGtesting.com
Printed in the USA
LVHW071411141222
735204LV00002B/4

* 9 7 8 0 9 7 7 7 2 6 4 2 4 *